new
literacies
q
AND DIGITAL EPISTEMOLOGIES

Colin Lankshear, Michele Knobel,
Chris Bigum, and Michael Peters
General Editors

Vol. 20

PETER LANG
New York • Washington, D.C./Baltimore • Bern
Frankfurt am Main • Berlin • Brussels • Vienna • Oxford

the power of the gaze